This book
belongs to

MOX

MOUSE WORKS

©1994 The Walt Disney Company
Printed in the United States of America

ISBN 1-57082-087-2
10 9 8 7 6 5

The sun came up over the African plain, hot and brilliant, just as it had done since the beginning of time.

Today, the first rays of the morning sun fell on an astonishing sight. Across the vast Pride Lands, animals moved in great herds, heading for a single destination.

Elephants plodded steadily. Antelope leaped through the grass. Giraffes loped. Cheetahs raced. Ants marched in a single line, while huge flocks of flamingoes winged across the sky.

They were all journeying to Pride Rock to celebrate the birth of King Mufasa's son.

Above the gathering, on the top of Pride Rock, Rafiki, the wise, old mystic, approached King Mufasa and Queen Sarabi. He cracked open a gourd, dipped his finger in the liquid, and made a special mark on the infant's forehead.

Then he carried the cub to the edge of the rock and held it high.

A loud cheer rose from the plain.
Elephants trumpeted. Monkeys
screeched. Zebras, rhinos, and a host
of other animals stamped their hooves.
Then a hush fell over the gathering.

Together, the animals of
Mufasa's kingdom knelt before Simba,
their new prince.

8

Yet one family member did not attend the ceremony. Mufasa's brother, Scar, had spent the entire morning toying with a mouse. He was just about to eat it when Zazu, the king's majordomo, appeared. Startled, Scar turned, and the mouse scampered away.

"Now look, Zazu, you've made me lose my lunch!" Scar complained.

"You'll lose more than that when the king gets through with you!"

But Scar wasn't listening. He was still hungry, and Zazu was beginning to look pretty tasty.

Scar pounced, but before he had
time to eat Zazu, a voice commanded,
"Drop him!"

Scar released the bird. "Why, if it isn't my big brother," he sneered.

"Sarabi and I didn't see you at the presentation of Simba," Mufasa said. "Is anything wrong?"

"That was today?" Scar said. "Oh, I feel simply awful! It must have slipped my mind."

"Well, as slippery as your mind is, you *are* the king's brother," Zazu reminded him.

Zazu also reminded Scar
that he should have been the first in
line to congratulate his brother.

"I *was* first in line until the little
hairball was born," retorted Scar.

"That 'hairball' is my son,"
Mufasa reminded him, "and your
future king."

"I shall practice my curtsy," Scar
said. Then he turned his back on them
and walked away.

The days passed, and Simba grew from an infant into a cub. One morning before dawn, Mufasa led Simba to the top of Pride Rock. As the sun edged over the horizon, Mufasa said, "Simba, look —everything the light touches is our kingdom. A king's time as ruler rises and falls like the sun. One day the sun will set on my time here and will rise with you as the new king."

"And this will all be mine? Wow!" said Simba, looking around. "But what about that shadowy place?"

Mufasa turned to his son. "That is beyond our borders. You must never go there, Simba."

As they wandered away from Pride Rock, Mufasa said, "Simba, everything you see exists together in a delicate balance. As king, you will need to understand that balance and respect all creatures because we are all connected in the great circle of life."

The young cub tried to listen, but a grasshopper caught his eye and he chased after it.

Just then Zazu arrived with the morning report. "Sire!" he addressed Mufasa. "Hyenas have crossed into the Pride Lands!"

Quickly the king ordered his majordomo to take Simba home.

"Aw, Dad, can't I come?" Simba whined.

"No, son," his father replied, and he took off after the dark shapes in the distance.

After Zazu made sure that Simba was home safely, the excited cub found Scar sunning himself on a rock. "Hey, Uncle Scar!" Simba cried. "My dad just showed me the whole kingdom, and I'm gonna rule it all!"

Scar scowled. Then, slowly, he began to smile. "So your father showed you the whole kingdom, did he? Did he show you what's beyond that rise at the border?"

"No," said Simba. "He said I can't go there."

"And he's absolutely right," Scar replied. "It's far too dangerous. Only the bravest of lions go there. An elephant graveyard is no place for a young prince."

"An elephant *what*?" said Simba. "Wow!"

"Oh, dear, I've said too much," said Scar, grinning slyly. "Just do me one favor?" he added. "Promise me that you'll never visit that dreadful place. And remember, it's our little secret."

As Scar backed away, Simba stared at the distant spot on the horizon. He had no idea that Scar had cleverly set a trap to rid himself of the future king . . . forever.

Simba knew that he would be disobeying his father if he went into the elephant graveyard. But hadn't Uncle Scar said that only the bravest of lions dared venture there? Wouldn't Dad be proud of such a brave cub? thought Simba.

Soon after, Simba went in search of his best friend Nala. He was happy to find Nala with her mother, Sarafina, and Queen Sarabi.

"Mom," he said to Sarabi, "I just heard about this great place! Can Nala and I go?"

"Where is this place, Simba?" his mother asked.

"Oh . . . near the waterhole!" the cub fibbed. Uncle Scar had said it was a secret.

"All right," said Sarabi, "as long as Zazu goes with you."

Not Zazu! thought Simba. He'll spoil everything!

As Zazu led the way, Simba whispered to Nala, "We've got to ditch him! We're not going to the waterhole. We're going to an elephant graveyard!"

When Zazu looked back and saw them whispering, he said, "Just look at you two! Your parents will be thrilled. One day, you two are going to be married! It's a tradition!"

"Marry her? Forget it!" said Simba. "I can't marry her. She's my best friend. And besides, when I'm king, I'll do just as I please!"

Zazu shook his head. "With that attitude, you'll be a pretty pathetic king!"

Simba laughed at Zazu. "I can't wait to be king!" the cub shouted, and he scampered away across the plains. Nala followed, and the two of them darted in and out of herds and escaped from Zazu.

"It worked! We lost Zazu!" said Simba, laughing.
"Now we can look for the elephant graveyard!"
In the spirit of victory, Simba playfully leapt
for Nala. But she was too quick for him and
flipped him onto his back. Together they
tumbled down a hill until they landed with
a thud. Next to them was a huge elephant skull.
   "This is it! We made it!" said Simba.
   "Wow!" exclaimed Nala. "It's really creepy."
   "C'mon," said Simba. "Let's check it out."

Before they could climb into the skull, Zazu caught up with them. "We're way beyond the boundary of the Pride Lands," he said. "And right now we all are in very real danger."

"I laugh in the face of danger!" said the brave lion cub. "Ha, ha!"

"Ha, ha!" replied the elephant skull. Then out of the skull's cavernous eyeholes popped three slobbering hyenas!

"Well, well, well, Banzai. What have we got here?" said one hyena.

"I don't know, Shenzi," answered another. "What do you think, Ed?"

Ed, the third hyena, just licked his lips and laughed.

Baring their fangs in wide grins, the hyenas crept toward the trespassers. They grabbed Zazu first.

"Why don't you pick on somebody your own size?" Simba shouted.

The hyenas dropped Zazu and raced after the cubs. When Shenzi threatened Nala, Simba swiped his claws across the hyena's nose.

The hyenas raced after the cubs, who found themselves trapped inside the bones of an elephant's rib cage. Then the angry hyenas advanced toward Simba, their sharp teeth gleaming.

A giant paw suddenly struck Shenzi, sending her and the other hyenas into a pile of bones.

No match for the powerful Lion King,
the beaten and bruised hyenas fled.
"Don't you ever come near my son
again!" Mufasa roared after them.

"Zazu!" Mufasa commanded. "Take Nala home. I have to teach my son a lesson."

As Simba sheepishly approached his father, Mufasa said, "Simba, I'm very disappointed in you."

"I was just trying to be brave, like you, Dad."

Mufasa tried to smile. "I'm only brave when I have to be. Simba, being brave doesn't mean you go looking for trouble."

Overhead, stars began to dot the evening sky. Simba looked at his father and said, "We'll always be together. Right?"

"Simba, let me tell you something my father told me: Look at the stars. The great kings of the past look down on us from those stars. They will always be there to guide you . . . and so will I."

Later that evening, Scar searched out the hyenas.

"Did you bring us anything to eat, Scar, old buddy?" Banzai asked.

"You don't really deserve this," said Scar, tossing them a chunk of meat. "I practically gift-wrapped those cubs for you, and you couldn't even dispose of them."

"What were we supposed to do—kill Mufasa?" said Banzai.

"Precisely," answered Scar.

As the hyenas ate ravenously, Scar thought of another plan. This time there would be no escape for Simba . . . or for his father.

The next day, Scar approached Simba. "Your father has a surprise for you," he said. Scar led the cub down the steep walls of a gorge.

"Will I like the surprise, Uncle Scar?"

"Simba, it's to *die* for. Now wait here and find out," Scar said, leaving Simba behind.

Not far from where Simba waited, a herd of wildebeests grazed. Not far from the herd, three hyenas waited, too. They were waiting for a signal from Scar. Shenzi saw him first. "There he is! Let's go!"

The hyenas ran toward the wildebeests. Sensing danger, the herd panicked and stampeded into the gorge, straight toward Simba.

Nearby, Mufasa and Zazu noticed the dust rising from the gorge. "Mufasa!" Scar yelled, appearing from behind a rock. "Quick! Stampede! Simba's down there!"

With no thought for his own safety, the Lion King leaped into the gorge and snatched the cub out of the path of the deadly hooves.

Mufasa jumped onto a rocky ledge and set Simba down.
Suddenly Mufasa felt the rocky wall crumble beneath his
hind paws. He fell back into the herd. Badly hurt, he tried to
climb another cliff. Looking up, he saw Scar.

"Brother . . . help me!" Mufasa pleaded.

Scar leaned toward Mufasa and pulled him close.

"Long live the king!" he whispered,
then let go. Mufasa lost his grip and disappeared
beneath the mass of moving animals.

Unaware of what Scar had done, Simba saw his father fall. When the wildebeests were gone, the cub raced down into the dust-filled gorge. There Simba found his father. He nuzzled the motionless body, but the great Lion King was dead.

Scar appeared beside Simba. "What have you done?" he said.

"He tried to save me!" the cub answered.

"If it weren't for you, your father would still be alive!" Scar snarled. "Run away, Simba . . . run away and never return!"

Confused and heartbroken, Simba began to run. He did not see the hyenas join Scar, or hear his uncle give the order to kill him.

At the edge of a plateau, the hyenas caught up with Simba. There was only one way for the lion cub to escape. He leaped off the plateau into a tangle of thorns.

The hyenas did not have the courage to follow. They could only stand at the edge of the plateau and jeer.

"If you ever come back, we'll kill you!" they shouted after him.

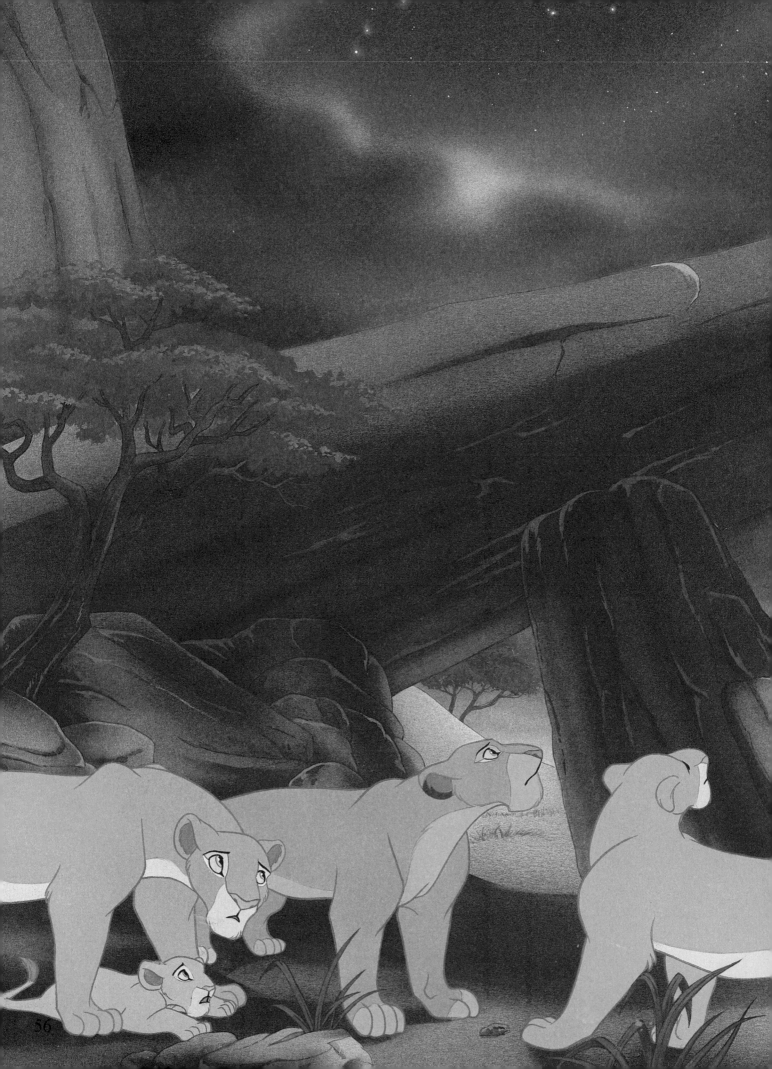

Certain that Simba had been killed, Scar returned to Pride Rock with the news.

"Mufasa died a hero," Scar solemnly announced. "He gave his own life to save his son. But, alas, both are dead."

Sarabi, Nala, and the other lionesses began to mourn. Scar slowly ascended Mufasa's throne. "It is with a heavy heart that I become your new king!"

Rafiki, shaking his head in disbelief, watched from a distance.

Injured and exhausted by his flight from the hyenas, Simba stumbled across the hot African wasteland. Above him, against the blazing midday sun, vultures circled. Unable to go farther, Simba fell to his knees and fainted.

When Simba opened his eyes again, the burning sun and the vultures were gone, but a meerkat and a warthog were standing over him.

"You okay, kid?" said the meerkat.

"You nearly died," said the warthog. "We saved you!"

"Thanks for your help," Simba replied. He stood on wobbly legs and started to leave.

The meerkat called after the shaky cub, "Where ya from?"

"It doesn't matter," Simba said quietly. Then he admitted, "I did something terrible . . . but I don't want to talk about it."

"Then you're an outcast!" cried the meerkat. "So are we! My name's Timon, and this is Pumbaa. Take my advice, kid. You gotta put your past behind you. No past, no future—no worries! *Hakuna matata!*"

With nowhere else to go, Simba followed Timon and Pumbaa to their jungle home. As Timon handed Simba some wriggling bugs to eat, the meerkat repeated, "This is the great life. No rules, no responsibilities, and—best of all—no worries!"

63

Time passed. In the carefree company of his new friends, Simba grew into a young lion.

One night, while the three of them were gazing at the stars, Simba said, "Someone once told me that the great kings of the past are up there, watching over us."

Pumbaa and Timon laughed. "Who'd have told ya a crazy thing like that?" said Timon.

Simba, thinking of his father, was silent.

The next day, as Simba was wandering through the jungle, he heard his friends shout for help.

Simba hurried toward the sound. Pumbaa was caught beneath the trunk of a fallen tree, and Timon was trying to protect him from a hungry young lioness.

As she leapt, Simba threw himself forward and knocked the lioness aside. For a moment, they tussled. Then the lioness pinned him to the ground and stared down at him.

"Simba?" she said hesitantly.

"Nala?" he replied.

As the lions hugged, Timon cried, "What's goin' on here?"

Simba laughed and introduced Nala to his friends. She smiled politely, but she could not stop staring at Simba. Finally she said, "Everyone thinks you're dead."

"They do?" Simba said.

"Yes. Scar told us about the stampede."

"What else did he tell you?" Simba asked cautiously.

"What else matters?" Nala exclaimed. "You're alive! And that means you're the king!"

"King?" cried Timon and Pumbaa in surprise.

Excusing themselves, Simba and Nala strolled into the jungle. "Scar let the hyenas take over the Pride Lands," Nala said. "Everything's destroyed. There's no food, no water. Simba, if you don't do something soon, everyone will starve."

"I can't go back," he insisted.

Nala did not understand why Simba refused to accept responsibility and help the Pride. "What's happened to you?" she asked. "You're not the Simba I remember."

"You're right. I'm not," he said. "Now are you satisfied?"

Before he turned to leave, Simba added angrily, "Listen! You think you can just show up and tell me how to live my life? You don't even know what I've been through."

Nala called after him, but Simba ignored her.

That night, while the others slept, Simba sat on a rock and gazed up at the twinkling sky. "I don't care what anybody says," he said aloud. "I won't go back. What would it prove, anyway? It won't change anything. You can't change the past."

Then Simba heard a strange sound. Somewhere in the jungle, someone was chanting in a singsong voice. As if from nowhere, the bent figure of an old baboon appeared.

"Who are you?" Simba asked, slightly annoyed.

"The question is: Who are *you*?" said the baboon.

Simba thought for a moment, then sighed.
The old baboon said, "I know your father."
"My father is dead," Simba replied.
"Nope!" said the baboon. "He's alive.
I'll show him to you. Just follow old Rafiki.
He knows the way."
The old baboon led Simba to a clear, smooth
pool. "Look down there," Rafiki advised.
In the pool, Simba saw only his reflection.
"Look *harder*," the baboon insisted.

A breeze rippled the water. When the pool became still, Simba stared at the face of his father.

"You see?" Rafiki said. "He lives in you!"

Simba heard a voice call his name, and he looked up and saw the image of his father in the stars.

"Look inside yourself, Simba," said his father's image. "You are more than what you have become. You must take your place in the circle of life. Remember who you are. . . . You are my son and the one true king. Remember . . . " The vision faded. Simba remained alone, thinking.

The next morning, Nala, Timon, and Pumbaa looked
all over for Simba. Finally Rafiki caught up with them.

"You won't find Simba here," the baboon said.
"The king has returned!"

Timon asked, "What do you mean?"

"He's gone back to challenge his uncle!"
Nala exclaimed.

Ahead of them, Simba moved swiftly toward Pride Rock.

As he crossed over into his homeland, he saw ruin and devastation everywhere.
For a moment, Simba hesitated. Then he felt a fresh wind and saw rain clouds
gathering on the horizon. With renewed hope, he continued his journey.

Soon Nala joined him, as did Pumbaa and even Timon. As they approached
Pride Rock, they saw some hyenas. Pumbaa and Timon stayed behind to
divert the pack. Nala went to find the lionesses, while Simba forged on
alone, in search of his mother.

Meanwhile, at Pride Rock, Scar reigned without shame.

"Where is your hunting party?" he shrieked at Sarabi.

"There is no food," she replied. "The herds have moved on. We have only one choice. We must leave Pride Rock."

"We're not going anywhere," he growled.

Sarabi replied, "Then you are sentencing us to death."

"Then so be it. I am the king, and I make the rules!"

"If you were half the king Mufasa was . . . " Sarabi began. Enraged, Scar struck her, and she fell.

A tremendous roar echoed among the rocks. Scar whirled and saw a great lion before him.

"Mufasa?" he said, gasping. "No! It can't be. You're dead." Weak and delirious, Scar backed away from the ghost. "What do you want?" he cried. "Why are you here? Go away. Go! Leave me alone!"

Although many years had passed, Sarabi still recognized her son. "Simba," she said quietly. "You're alive!"

"Simba!" Scar exclaimed. Then he glared at the hyenas, who had failed to kill Mufasa's boy.

"This is my kingdom," Simba proclaimed. "Step down, Scar."

Scar laughed. "Well, I would, of course. But there is one little problem." He gestured toward the hyenas.

Quickly the hyenas swarmed over Simba.

"Enough!" Scar finally cried. The hyenas drew back, providing a clear path for Scar to approach Simba, who struggled to avoid falling to his death.

Scar sneered. "Where have I seen this before? Oh, yes . . . I remember. That's just the way your father looked before I killed him."

Gathering all his strength, Simba leapt toward his uncle. As they fought, Scar ordered the hyenas to help him.

Moments later Nala and the lionesses arrived, along with Timon and Pumbaa. With fury, they attacked the hyenas, attempting to drive them away.

As the groups clashed, lightning struck the dry grass of the flatlands. The wind, now fierce, swept huge flames toward Pride Rock. During the battle, Simba, became separated from his uncle.

Then Simba saw Scar crawling up Pride Rock. Simba dashed up the steep face, dodging fire and smoke. This time, he trapped Scar at the edge.

"Simba, you don't understand," Scar insisted. "I didn't kill your father. It was the hyenas. They are the enemy. Now that you're back . . . together, we can defeat them!"

"Run away, Scar," Simba commanded, repeating the advice his uncle had once given him. "Run away and never return!"

Scar started to slink away, but then he turned and lunged for Simba. Acting swiftly, Simba hurled Scar off the cliff. The sound of hungry hyenas drifted up from the gorge, revealing Scar's awful fate.

As rain began to fall, Simba climbed to the top of Pride Rock. Then the clouds parted, revealing a star-filled sky. Simba roared triumphantly, and all who heard him reacted with joy.

Soon, under the rule of a wise and brave king, the Pride Lands flourished. The herds returned to graze, and food was plentiful once again.

Soon the animals gathered once more to celebrate the birth of a king's son. Simba and Nala watched proudly as Rafiki held their new cub high over Pride Rock.

As the morning sun touched the African plain, Simba thought of something his father had once told him. "A king's time as ruler rises and falls like the sun. One day the sun will set on my time and rise with you as the new king."

Someday Simba would pass on these same words to his own son . . . continuing the unbroken circle of life.